LEGENDARY

POKÉMON

THE ESSENTIAL GUIDE
SINNOH EDITION

By Katherine Fang

Scholastic Inc.

New York   Toronto   London   Auckland   Sydney

Mexico City   New Delhi   Hong Kong   Buenos Aires

ISBN-10: 0-545-16023-5
ISBN-13: 978-0-545-16023-0

© 2009 Pokémon. © 1997–2009 Nintendo, Creatures,
GAME FREAK, TV Tokyo, ShoPro, JR Kikaku.
Pokémon properties are trademarks of Nintendo. All rights reserved.

Published by Scholastic Inc.
SCHOLASTIC and associated logos are trademarks and/or registered trademarks of Scholastic Inc.

12 11 10 9 8 7 6 5 4 3 2 1   9 10 11 12 13 14/0

Designed by Cheung Tai
Printed in the U.S.A.
First printing, July 2009

LEGENDARY POKÉMON

Pokémon from a parallel world . . .
Psychic Pokémon hidden beneath a lake . . .
Pokémon with power over space and time . . .

There's only one place where you will meet all these Pokemon:

Sinnoh!

Every part of the Pokémon world has its myths and legends. The Sinnoh Region is rich with tales of the Legendary Pokémon who live there. From Azelf to Uxie, all of these Pokémon have a special place in their world. This book holds the secrets of these special Pokémon and the legends they have inspired.

It's time to discover the Legendary Pokémon of Sinnoh!

AZELF

PRONOUNCED: (AZ-ELF)

SPECIES: Willpower Pokémon

Height: 1' 00"
Weight: 0.7 LBS.

TYPE:

PSYCHIC

In Sinnoh, Azelf is known as the being of willpower. Without willpower, people and Pokémon would have no energy to act. That makes Azelf a very important Pokémon!

Azelf is linked to two other Pokémon, Mesprit and Uxie. All three Pokémon may have come from the same Egg. They may also be part of the Sinnoh Space-Time Legend, a tale that describes how the world was formed. If the Space-Time Legend is true, that makes Azelf a very ancient Pokémon.

Now Azelf, Mesprit, and Uxie live below Sinnoh's lakes. The lake in the west is called Lake Valor, and that is where Azelf can be found. Even while it sleeps, it helps maintain the world's balance.

FUN FACT

Azelf is a small Pokémon, but it contains great power. Together with Mesprit and Uxie, Azelf can calm Dialga and Palkia!

CRESSELIA

PRONOUNCED: (CRES-SEL-ee-uh)

SPECIES: Lunar Pokémon

Height: 4' 11"
Weight: 188.7 LBS.

Like many Pokémon, Cresselia is connected to nature. People say that Cresselia symbolizes the crescent moon, and its body does have a crescent shape. It can even use Lunar Dance, its special move, to heal other Pokémon. Cresselia's wings give off shiny particles, and its tail has an aurora when the moon is right.

Many Legendary Pokémon are extremely powerful. If just one of them is out of control, it could cause chaos! However, Legendary Pokémon will often balance out other Legendary Pokémon. Cresselia and Darkrai are a good example of this natural order. Cresselia has the power to confront Darkrai and calm the nightmares that Darkrai creates.

FUN FACT

Is it a boy or a girl? With most Legendary Pokémon, it's hard to tell. But Cresselia is always a female!

DARKRAI

PRONOUNCED: (DARK-RYE)

SPECIES: Pitch-Black Pokémon

Height: 4' 11"
Weight: 111.3 LBS.

TYPE:

DARK

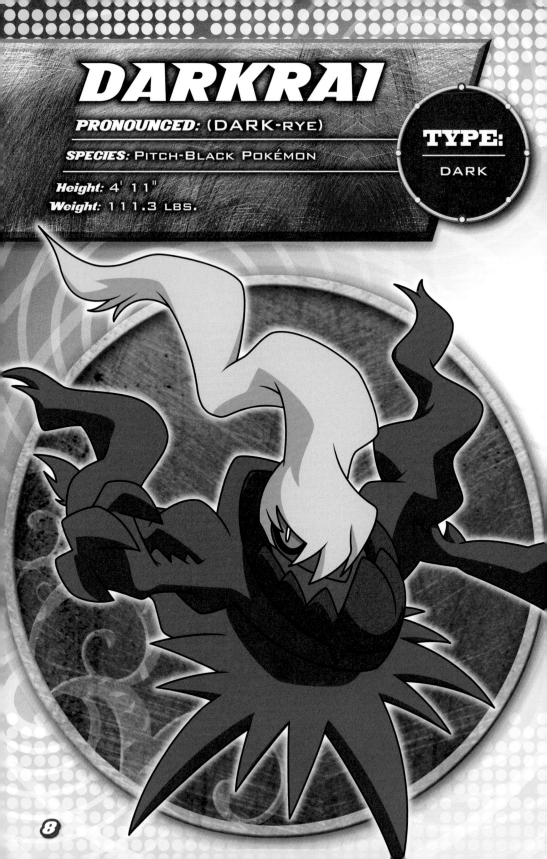

Darkrai is a Pokémon with a scary reputation. That's because Darkrai is associated with nightmares! Stories say that Darkrai gives people nightmares on moonless nights.

While Darkrai doesn't mean to hurt others, it does have fearsome powers. Darkrai's special move, Dark Void, can put several targets to sleep at the same time. Its Bad Dreams ability will give them nightmares, too!

On nights when there's a new moon, the moon can't be seen. These are the nights when Darkrai is active, but it is still hard to spot. Darkrai can fly and often disappears into the shadows to avoid being seen. Sometimes Darkrai will communicate with people using dreams or human language.

FUN FACT

Can a piece of jewelry protect people from nightmares? Some people think so. If Darkrai is nearby, they wear Lunar Wing charms to keep bad dreams at bay.

DIALGA

PRONOUNCED: (DEE-AL-GUH)

SPECIES: Temporal Pokémon

Height: 17' 09"
Weight: 1505.8 LBS.

TYPE:

STEEL
DRAGON

Travelers in Sinnoh will encounter statues of two powerful Pokémon: Dialga and Palkia. There are many myths about these two. People believe that Dialga controls time. They say that time started when Dialga first appeared.

Dialga does have the power to affect time, and the Roar of Time is its special attack. When it uses the Roar of Time, the blue jewel on its chest glows.

Most people in Sinnoh have only seen statues of Dialga. This Pokémon is hard to spot in the wild because it likes to live in another dimension. In that dimension, Dialga is territorial, and it fights to protect its turf. So if Dialga meets Palkia, the two of them will battle!

FUN FACT

Sinnoh is home to a rare treasure called the Adamant Orb. This strange orb can make Dialga even more powerful.

GIRATINA
ALTERED FORME

PRONOUNCED: (GEAR-UH-TEE-na AL-terd form)

SPECIES: Renegade Pokémon

Height: 14' 09"
Weight: 1653.5 lbs.

TYPE:
GHOST
DRAGON

Some of Sinnoh's Legendary Pokémon don't even live in Sinnoh. Instead, these Legendary Pokémon live in other dimensions. Giratina lives in the Reverse World, a strange place with low gravity. Giratina is the only one who is free to travel between the Reverse World and the normal world. These two worlds are linked. When time and space are damaged, the Reverse World corrects the damage. But if Giratina sees someone cause lots of damage to time and space, it will chase down the offender!

FUN FACT

Giratina can see the normal world from inside the Reverse World.

HEATRAN

PRONOUNCED: (HEE-tran)

SPECIES: Lava Dome Pokémon

Height: 5' 07"
Weight: 948.0 lbs.

TYPE:
FIRE
STEEL

Heatran stands nearly as tall as a person, but it weighs a lot more — nearly half a ton! Even though it is heavy, this Pokémon can climb up cavern walls and ceilings thanks to the special shape of its feet. Each foot is shaped like a cross, and that helps it grab onto rocky surfaces. Heatran can then crawl around the volcanic caverns where it lives.

This Pokémon likes it hot, and its body is highly adapted to its habitat. Heatran has the Flash Fire ability, which protects it from fire. Attack Heatran with fire and its Flash Fire ability will just make it more powerful!

FUN FACT

Heatran can use fire to attack, too. Its special move, Magma Storm, heats things up for its foes.

MANAPHY

PRONOUNCED: (MAN-A-PHEE)

SPECIES: Seafaring Pokémon

Height: 1' 00"
Weight: 3.1 LBS.

TYPE:

WATER

Why is Manaphy called the Seafaring Pokémon? It must be because this tiny Pokémon migrates across oceans. It knows the way to the sea floor where it was hatched, and can travel long distances to return there. Manaphy's body is also eighty percent water. That makes this Pokémon a true creature of the sea.

With its big eyes and cute body, Manaphy looks more like a teeny-tiny Pokémon than a Legendary one. But looks aren't everything! When Manaphy is in danger, it can use the Heart Swap move to protect itself. Heart Swap will switch Manaphy's condition with that of another being. Only Manaphy can learn this special move.

FUN FACT

Manaphy can use Heart Swap to share its strength with someone else. Heart Swap can even exchange two people's minds!

MESPRIT

PRONOUNCED: (MES-prit)

SPECIES: Emotion Pokémon

Height: 1' 00"
Weight: 0.7 LBS.

TYPE:

PSYCHIC

In Sinnoh, Mesprit is known as the Being of Emotion. Legends say that Mesprit taught people the importance of both good and bad emotions. That was a long time ago, and now Mesprit sleeps beneath Lake Verity, not far from Twinleaf Town.

Even though Mesprit is asleep, it can still see what goes on around it. Mesprit's spirit can separate from its body and fly around the lake. Is Mesprit behind the glowing, ghostly figure that sometimes appears at Lake Verity?

Mesprit, Azelf, and Uxie are a special trio. However, the special qualities that link these three Pokémon can make them a target. These Pokémon are keys to unlocking Sinnoh's ancient secrets. No wonder they prefer to stay hidden!

FUN FACT

It's never a good idea to disturb a Legendary Pokémon. If the rumors are true, a person who messes with Mesprit will lose all emotion!

PALKIA

PRONOUNCED: (PAL-KEE-UH)

SPECIES: Spacial Pokémon

Height: 13' 09"

Weight: 740.8 LBS.

TYPE:

WATER

DRAGON

What Pokémon could be strong enough to warp space? It's the Legendary Pokémon Palkia! When people say that Palkia controls space, they don't mean that Palkia controls stars and planets. According to Sinnoh legend, Palkia has power over the dimension of space itself! This Legendary Pokémon can easily travel between dimensions. It can pull parts of the normal world into another dimension, too.

Palkia lives in a parallel dimension and rarely appears in Sinnoh. That may be a good thing, because its powers could cause a lot of trouble! One of Palkia's powerful attacks is called Spatial Rend. When it uses this move, the pearly gems on its shoulders will glow.

FUN FACT

The Lustrous Orb is a unique jewel that is found in Sinnoh. This Orb has a special effect on Palkia's powers.

REGIGIGAS

PRONOUNCED: (REDGE-EE-GEE-GUS)

SPECIES: Colossal Pokémon

Height: 12' 02"
Weight: 925.9 LBS.

TYPE:

NORMAL

Regigigas has a connection to three Pokémon called Regirock, Registeel, and Regice. They have different types, but these Pokémon are like Regigigas in many ways. All of them have robotic voices and flashing lights on their bodies. They are all found in old and forgotten places.

Is Regigigas some kind of ancient guardian? Nobody knows, but Regigigas must have been around for a long time. It lives in hidden ruins, where it sits as still as a statue. If the land is in danger, Regigigas may awaken to protect the land. It will also attack intruders if it is disturbed.

FUN FACT

Regigigas is not a fast Pokémon, but it is famous for its strength. Legends say it uses ropes to pull entire continents!

SHAYMIN
LAND FORME

PRONOUNCED: (SHAY-MIN LAND FORM)

SPECIES: Gratitude Pokémon

Height: 0' 08"
Weight: 4.6 LBS.

TYPE:

GRASS

Shaymin is a Pokémon that can clean its environment. Shaymin absorbs toxins into its body, then purifies the toxins and turns them into light and water. Its Seed Flare move creates an explosion that releases this light and water. The more toxins Shaymin absorbs, the more powerful its Seed Flare move will be.

Shaymin's Land Forme is very shy. When it feels happy, it makes flowers bloom on its back. When it absorbs toxins, its flowers turn gray. The flowers look like the Gracedia flowers that grow in Sinnoh.

Shaymin can use flowers to camouflage itself. Because of the blossoms that grow on its back, Shaymin blends right into any flowery environment.

UXIE

PRONOUNCED: (YUKE-SEE)

SPECIES: KNOWLEDGE POKÉMON

Height: 1' 00"
Weight: 0.7 LBS.

TYPE:

PSYCHIC

Where does knowledge come from? Some people in Sinnoh believe it comes from Uxie. There is a legend that says when Uxie appeared, people gained intelligence. They used this intelligence to improve their lives. Now Uxie is known as the Being of Knowledge. It sounds like Uxie has a high IQ, but no one has ever measured it! Like Azelf and Mesprit, Uxie may have emerged even before people existed.

Anyone who looks for Uxie should first seek knowledge of how to swim — and they might also want to find a warm coat! Lake Acuity is in northern Sinnoh, where the weather is frosty. Local stories describe a Legendary Pokémon who appears above the lake, and that Pokémon sounds like Uxie itself.

FUN FACT

Why are Uxie's eyes closed? It has the power to grant knowledge, but it has the power to erase knowledge, too. Legends say that Uxie can erase the memory of anyone who sees its eyes!

GIRATINA
ORIGIN FORME

PRONOUNCED: (GEAR-UH-TEE-NA OR-UH-JUN FORM)

SPECIES: RENEGADE POKÉMON

Height: 22' 07"
Weight: 1433.0 LBS.

TYPE:
GHOST
DRAGON

Giratina uses its Origin Forme to fly in the Reverse World. When it enters the normal world, it changes to Altered Forme. Why does Giratina have two formes? Altered Forme may help it adapt to the normal world, where gravity is stronger than in the Reverse World.

FUN FACT

Giratina is the only Ghost-and-Dragon-type Pokémon.

SHAYMIN
SKY FORME

TYPE: GRASS FLYING

PRONOUNCED: (SHAY-MIN SKY FORM)

SPECIES: GRATITUDE POKÉMON

Height: 1' 04"
Weight: 11.4 LBS.

Shaymin Sky Forme is much bolder than its Land Forme. In fact, its personality is almost the exact opposite of its Land Forme. Both Formes have the same power to clean the environment.

So how does Shaymin transform from Sky Forme into Land Forme? Gracedia flowers help. Every year Shaymin Land Forme gather in a field of Gracedia flowers. There they transform into Sky Forme and fly off to find a new home. A new flower garden grows wherever they land.

FUN FACT

Gracedia flowers are special to Sinnoh's people, too. They give Gracedia bouquets as a gift of gratitude. These bouquets look just like the Gratitude Pokémon!

LEGENDARY QUIZ

Ready to prove you're an EXPERT on Sinnoh's Legendary Pokémon? See if you can answer these questions! Give yourself ten points for every correct answer.

1. What item do people use to keep Darkrai from giving them nightmares?

_____

2. Which three Legendary Pokémon are said to have come from the same Egg?

_____

3. Palkia and Dialga are the Pokémon who represent what two forces?

_____

4. What move does Shaymin use to purify toxins?

_____

5. Why does Uxie keep its eyes closed?

_____

6. What special body part helps Heatran climb on cavern walls and ceilings?

_____

7. What species of Pokémon is Regigigas?

_____

8. What is Cresselia said to represent?

_____

9. How much of Manaphy's body is made of water?

_____

10. What is Giratina's unique move?

_____

ANSWERS

1. Lunar Wing .
2. Azelf, Mesprit, and Uxie
3. Space and time
4. Seed Flare
5. Uxie can erase the memory of anyone who sees its eyes.
6. Cross-shaped feet
7. Colossal Pokémon
8. Crescent moon
9. Eighty percent
10. It can travel between the normal world and the Reverse World.

SCORING

80 and above
Congratulations! You know so much about Legendary Pokémon, you could become a professor!

60 to 70
Nice work! You just might have what it takes to become a full-fledged Pokémon Trainer.

50 and below
Hmmm . . . you may want to review this book one more time before exploring Sinnoh. But keep at it—becoming a Pokémon Trainer takes a lot of hard work and practice.